"*If you want your children to be intelligent, read them fairy tales.*
If you want them to be more intelligent, read them more fairy tales."

– Albert Einstein

To our mother, who wanted us all to be intelligent.

FAMILY TREASURY OF CLASSIC TALES

ONCE UPON A TIME

LITTLE RED RIDING HOOD

◆

THE BRAVE LITTLE TAILOR

◆

THE ELVES AND THE SHOEMAKER

◆

RAPUNZEL

DESIGNED BY
JONAS BELL

LITTLE RED RIDING HOOD

ONCE upon a time there lived in a certain village a little country girl, the prettiest creature who was ever seen. Her mother was excessively fond of her; and her grandmother doted on her still more. This good woman had a little red riding hood made for her. It suited the girl so extremely well that everybody called her Little Red Riding Hood.

One day her mother, having made some cakes, said to her, "Go, my dear, and see how your grandmother is doing for I hear she has been very ill. Take her a cake and a little pot of butter."

Little Red Riding Hood set out immediately to go to her grandmother, who lived in another village.

As she was going through the wood, she met with a wolf, who had a very great mind to eat her up, but he dared not, because of some woodcutters working nearby in the forest. He asked her where she was going. The poor child, who did not know that it was dangerous to stay and talk to a wolf, said to him, "I am going to see my grandmother and carry her a cake and a little pot of butter from my mother."

"Does she live far off?" said the wolf.

"Oh I say," answered Little Red Riding Hood." It is beyond that mill you see there, at the first house in the village."

"Well," said the wolf, "and I'll go and see her too. I'll go this way and go you that, and we shall see who will be there first."

The wolf ran as fast as he could, taking the shortest path, and the little girl took a roundabout way, entertaining herself by gathering nuts, running after butterflies, and gathering bouquets of little flowers. It was not long before the wolf arrived at the old woman's house. He knocked at the door: tap, tap.

"Who's there?"

"Your grandchild, Little Red Riding Hood," replied the wolf, mimicking her voice; "who has brought you a cake and a little pot of butter sent you by mother."

The good grandmother, who was in bed, because she was somewhat ill, cried out, "Pull the bobbin, and the latch will go up."

The wolf pulled the bobbin, and the door opened. As soon as Grandmother saw the wolf she sprang from her bed and ran out the back door of her cottage. The wolf then shut the door and got into the grandmother's bed, expecting Little Red Riding Hood, who came some time afterwards and knocked at the door: tap, tap.

"Who's there?"

Little Red Riding Hood, hearing the big voice of the wolf, was at first afraid; but believing her grandmother had a cold and was hoarse, answered, "It is your grandchild Little Red Riding Hood, who has brought you a cake and a little pot of butter mother sends you."

The wolf cried out to her, softening his voice as much as he could, "Pull the bobbin, and the latch will go up."

Little Red Riding Hood pulled the bobbin, and the door opened.

The wolf, seeing her come in, said to her, hiding himself under the bedclothes, "Put the cake and the little pot of butter upon the stool, and come sit by my bed."

Little Red Riding Hood pulled a chair up beside her Grandmother's bed. She was greatly amazed to see how her grandmother looked in her nightclothes, and said to her,

"Grandmother, what big arms you have!"

"All the better to hug you with, my dear."

"Grandmother, what big ears you have!"

"All the better to hear with, my child."

"Grandmother, what big eyes you have!"

"All the better to see with, my child."

"Grandmother, what big teeth you have got!"

"All the better to eat you up with."

The wolf sprang out of bed ready to lunge at Red Riding Hood, when the door flew open and there stood Red Riding Hood's father – one shot from his gun and the wolf ran out the back door howling as he went. Fortunately, for Red Riding Hood, her grandmother had run to her father who was hunting in the woods nearby. So that afternoon Red Riding Hood, her father and her grandmother all enjoyed the delicious cakes and butter and the wolf was never heard from again.

THE BRAVE LITTLE TAILOR

ne summer morning a little tailor was sitting at his table near the window. In good spirits, he was sewing with all his might. A peasant woman came down the street crying, "Good jam for sale! Good jam for sale!"

That sounded good to the little tailor, so he stuck his dainty head out of the window and shouted, "Come up here, my dear woman! You can sell your goods here!"

The woman carried her heavy basket up the three flights of stairs to the tailor, who had her unpack all of her jars. He examined them, picking each one up and holding it to his nose. Finally he said, "This jam looks good to me. Weigh out four ounces for me, even if it comes to a quarter pound."

The woman, who had hoped to make a good sale, gave him what he asked for, then went away angry and grumbling.

"May God bless this jam to give me health and strength," said the little tailor. Then taking a loaf of bread from his cupboard, he cut himself a large slice and spread it with the jam. "That is not going to taste bad," he said, "but I will finish the jacket before I bite into it."

He laid the bread aside and continued his sewing, happily making his stitches larger and larger. Meanwhile, the smell of the sweet jam rose to the wall where a large number of flies were sitting. Attracted by the smell, a swarm of them settled onto the bread.

"Hey! Who invited you?" said the little tailor, driving away the unbidden guests. However, the flies, who did not understand him, would not be turned away, and they came back in ever-increasing numbers. Finally, losing his temper, he reached for a piece of cloth and shouted, "Now I'm going to give it to you!" then hit at them without mercy. When he backed off and counted, there were no fewer than seven of them lying dead before him, with their legs stretched out.

"Aren't you someone?" he said to himself, surprised at his own bravery. The whole town shall hear about this." He hastily cut out a banner for himself, then embroidered on it with large letters, Seven with one blow. "The town?" he said further. "The whole world shall hear about this!" And his heart jumped for joy like a lamb's tail.

The tailor tied the banner around his body and set forth into the world, for he thought that his workshop was too small for such bravery. Before leaving he looked about his house for something that he could take with him. Finding nothing but a piece of old cheese, he put that into his pocket. Outside the town gate he found a bird that was caught in a bush. It went into his pocket with the cheese.

He bravely took to the road, and being light and agile he did not grow weary. The road led him up a mountain, and when he reached the top a huge giant was sitting there, looking around contentedly.

The little tailor went up to him cheerfully and said, "Good day, friend. Are you just sitting here looking at the wide world? I am on my way out there to prove myself. Do you want to come with me?"

The giant looked at the tailor with contempt, saying, "You wretch! You miserable fellow!"

"You don't say!" answered the little tailor. Unbuttoning his coat, he showed the banner to the giant. "You can read what kind of man I am."

The giant read Seven with one blow, and thinking that the tailor had killed seven men, he gained some respect for the little fellow. But he did want to put him to the test, so he picked up a stone and squeezed it with his hand until water dripped from it.

"Do what I just did," said the giant, "if you have the strength."

"Is that all?" said the little tailor. "That is child's play for someone like me." Reaching into his pocket he pulled out the soft cheese and squeezed it until liquid ran from it. "That was even better, wasn't it?" he said.

The giant did not know what to say, for he did not believe the little man. Then the giant picked up a stone and threw it so high that it could scarcely be seen. "Now, you little dwarf, do that."

"A good throw," said the tailor, "but the stone did fall back to earth. I'll

throw one for you that will not come back." He reached into his pocket, pulled out the bird, and threw it into the air. Happy to be free, the bird flew up and away, and did not come back. "How did you like that, friend?" asked the tailor.

"You can throw well enough," said the giant, but now let's see if you are able to carry anything proper." He led the little tailor to a mighty oak tree that had been cut down and was lying on the ground. He said, "If you are strong enough, then help me carry this tree out of the woods."

"Gladly," answered the little man. "You take the trunk on your shoulder, and I will carry the branches and twigs. After all, they are the heaviest."

The giant lifted the trunk onto his shoulder, but the tailor sat down on a branch, and the giant, who could not see behind himself, had to drag along the entire tree, with the little tailor sitting on top. Cheerful and in good spirits, he whistled the song "There Were Three Tailors Who Rode Out to the Gate," as though carrying a tree were child's play.

The giant, after dragging the heavy load a little way, could not go any further, and he called out, "Listen, I have to drop the tree."

The tailor jumped down, took hold of the tree with both arms, as though he had been carrying it, and said to the giant, "You are such a big fellow, and you can't even carry a tree."

They walked on together until they came to a cherry tree. The giant took hold of the treetop where the ripest fruit was hanging, bent it down, and put it into the tailor's hand, inviting him to eat. However, the little tailor

was much too weak to hold the tree, and when the giant let go, the tree sprang upward, throwing the tailor into the air. When he fell back to earth, without injury, the giant said, "What? You don't have enough strength to hold that little switch?"

"There is no lack of strength," answered the little tailor. "Do you think that that would be a problem for someone who killed seven with one blow? I jumped over the tree because hunters are shooting down there in the brush. Jump over it yourself, if you can."

The giant made the attempt, but could not clear the tree and got stuck in the branches. So the little tailor kept the upper hand here as well.

The giant said, "If you are such a brave fellow, then come with me to our cave and spend the night with us."

The little tailor agreed and followed him. When they reached the cave, other giants were sitting there by a fire. Each one had a roasted sheep in his hand and was eating it. The little tailor looked around and thought, "It is a lot more roomy here than in my workshop."

The giant showed him a bed and told him to lie down and go to sleep. However, the little tailor found the bed too large, so instead of lying there he crept into a corner. At midnight the giant thought that the little tailor was fast asleep, so he got up, took a large iron bar, and with a single blow smashed the bed in two. He thought he had put an end to the grasshopper.

Early the next morning the giants went into the woods, having completely forgotten the little tailor, when he suddenly approached them cheerfully and boldly. Fearing that he would strike them all dead, the terrified giants ran away in haste.

The little tailor continued on his way, always following his pointed nose. After wandering a long time, he came to the courtyard of a royal palace, and being tired, he lay down in the grass and fell asleep. While he was lying there people came and looked at him from all sides, and they read his banner, Seven with one blow.

"Oh," they said, "what is this great war hero doing here in the midst of peace? He must be a powerful lord."

They went and reported him to the king, thinking that if war were to break out, he would be an important and useful man who at any price should not be allowed to go elsewhere. The king was pleased with this advice, and he sent one of his courtiers to the little tailor to offer him a position in the army, as soon as he woke up.

The messenger stood by the sleeper and waited until he stretched his arms and legs and opened his eyes, and then he delivered his offer.

"That is precisely why I came here," answered the little tailor. "I am ready to enter the king's service." Thus he was received with honor and given a special place to live.

However, the soldiers were opposed to the little tailor, and wished that he were a thousand miles away. "What will happen," they said amongst themselves, "if we quarrel with him, and he strikes out against us? Seven of us will fall with each blow. People like us cannot stand up to that."

So they came to a decision, and all together they went to the king and asked to be released. "We were not made," they said, "to stand up to a man who kills seven with one blow."

The king needed a plan. He would like to be rid of the little tailor, but he did not dare dismiss him. He was afraid that this new stranger would kill him and all of his people, and then set himself on the throne.

He thought long and hard, and finally found an answer. He sent a message to the little tailor, informing him that because he was such a great war hero he would make him an offer. In a forest in his country there lived two giants who were causing great damage with robbery, murder, pillage, and arson. No one could approach the two giants without placing themselves in mortal danger. If he could conquer and kill these two giants, the king would give him his only daughter to wife and half his kingdom for a dowry. Furthermore, a hundred horsemen would go with him for support.

"That is something for a man like you," thought the little tailor. "It is not every day that someone is offered a beautiful princess and half a kingdom."

"Yes," he replied. "I shall conquer the giants, but I do not need the hundred horsemen. Anyone who can strike down seven with one blow has no cause to be afraid of two."

The little tailor set forth, and the hundred horsemen followed him. At the edge of the forest, he said to them, "You stay here. I shall take care of the giants myself."

Leaping into the woods, he looked to the left and to the right. He soon saw the two giants. They were lying asleep under a tree, snoring until the branches bent up and down. The little tailor, not lazy, filled both pockets with stones and climbed the tree. Once in the middle of the tree, he slid out on a branch until he was seated right above the sleepers. Then he dropped one stone after another onto one giant's chest. For a long time the giant did not feel anything, but finally he woke up, shoved his companion, and said, "Why are you hitting me?"

"You are dreaming," said the other one. "I am not hitting you."

They fell asleep again, and the tailor threw a stone at the second one.

"What is this?" said the other one. "Why are you throwing things at me?"

"I am not throwing anything at you," answered the first one, grumbling.

They quarreled for a while, but because they were tired, they made peace, and they both closed their eyes again. Then the little tailor began his game again. Choosing his largest stone, he threw it at the first giant with all his strength, hitting him in the chest.

"That is too mean!" shouted the giant, then jumped up like a madman and pushed his companion against the tree, until it shook. The other one paid him back in kind, and they became so angry that they pulled up trees and struck at each other until finally, at the same time, they both fell to the ground dead.

Then the little tailor jumped down. "It is fortunate," he said, "that they did not pull up the tree where I was sitting, or I would have had to jump into another one like a squirrel. But people like me are nimble."

Drawing his sword, he gave each one a few good blows to the chest, then went back to the horsemen and said, "The work is done. I finished off both of them, but it was hard. In their need they pulled up trees to defend themselves. But it didn't help them, not against someone like me who kills seven with one blow."

"Are you not wounded?" asked the horsemen.

"Everything is all right," answered the tailor. "They did not so much as bend one of my hairs."

Not wanting to believe him, the horesmen rode into the woods. There they found the giants swimming in their own blood, and all around lay the uprooted trees.

The little tailor asked the king for the promised reward, but the latter regretted the promise, and once again he began to think of a way to get the hero off his neck. "Before you receive my daughter and half the kingdom," he said, "you must fulfill another heroic deed. In the woods there is a unicorn that is causing much damage. First you must capture it."

"I am even less afraid of a unicorn than I was of two giants. Seven with one blow, that is my thing."

Taking a rope and an ax, he went into the woods. Once again he told those who went with him to wait behind. He did not have to look very long. The unicorn soon appeared, leaping toward the tailor as if it wanted to spear him at once.

"Gently, gently," said the tailor. "Not so fast." He stopped, waited until the animal was very near, then jumped behind a tree. The unicorn ran with all its might into the tree, sticking its horn so tightly into the trunk that it did not have enough strength to pull it out again, and thus it was captured.

"Now I have the little bird," said the tailor, coming out from behind the tree. First he tied the rope around the unicorn's neck, then he cut the horn out of the tree with the ax. When everything was ready, he led the animal away and brought it to the king who now – whether he wanted to or not – had to keep his promise and give him his daughter and half the kingdom. If he had known that it was not a war hero, but rather a little tailor standing before him, it would have been quite painful for him.

The wedding was thus held with great ceremony and celebrated by all the kingdom.

And thus the little tailor was a king, and he remained a king as long as he lived.

THE ELVES AND THE SHOEMAKER

There was once a shoemaker, who worked very hard and was very honest: but still he could not earn enough to live upon; and at last all he had in the world was gone, save just enough leather to make one pair of shoes.

Then he cut his leather out, all ready to make up the next day, meaning to rise early in the morning to his work. His conscience was clear and his heart light amidst all his troubles; so he went peaceably to bed, left all his cares to Heaven, and soon fell asleep. In the morning after he had said his prayers, he sat himself down to his work; when, to his great wonder, there stood the shoes already made, upon the table. The good man knew not what to say or think at such an odd thing happening. He looked at the workmanship; there was not one false stitch in the whole job; all was so neat and true, that it was quite a masterpiece.

The same day a customer came in, and the shoes suited him so well that he willingly paid a price higher than usual for them; and the poor shoemaker, with the money, bought leather enough to make two pairs more. In the evening he cut out the work, and went to bed early, that he might get up and begin early the next day; but he was saved all the trouble, for when he got up in the morning the work was done ready to his hand. Soon in came buyers, who paid him handsomely for his goods, so that he bought leather enough for four pair more. He cut out the work again overnight and found it done in the morning, as before; and so it went on for some time: what was prepared in the evening was always done by daybreak, and the good man soon became thriving and well off again.

One evening, about Christmas-time, as he and his wife were sitting over the fire chatting together, he said to her, "I should like to sit up and watch tonight, that we may see who it is that comes and does my work for me." The wife liked the thought; so they left a light burning, and hid themselves in a corner of the room, behind a curtain that was hung up there, and watched what would happen.

As soon as it was midnight, there came in two little naked elves; and they sat themselves upon the shoemaker's bench, took up all the work that was cut out, and began to ply with their little fingers, stitching and rapping and tapping away at such a rate, that the shoemaker was all wonder, and could not take his eyes off them. And on they went, till the job was quite done, and the shoes stood ready for use upon the table. This was long before daybreak; and then they bustled away as quick as lightning.

The next day the wife said to the shoemaker. "These little elves have made us rich, and we ought to be thankful to them, and do them a good turn if we can. I am quite sorry to see them run about as they do; and indeed it is not very decent, for they have nothing upon their backs to keep off the cold. I'll tell you what, I will make each of them a shirt, and a coat and waistcoat, and a pair of pantaloons into the bargain; and you make each of them a little pair of shoes."

About midnight in they came, dancing and skipping, hopped round the room, and then went to sit down to their work as usual; but when they saw the clothes lying for them, they laughed and chuckled, and seemed delighted.

Then they dressed themselves in the twinkling of an eye, and danced and capered and sprang about, as merry as could be; till at last they danced out the door, and away over the green.

The good couple saw them no more; but everything went well with them from that time forward, as long as they lived.

RAPUNZEL

ONCE upon a time there lived a man and his wife who were very unhappy because they had no children. These good people had a little window at the back of their house, which looked into the most lovely garden, full of all manner of beautiful flowers and vegetables; but the garden was surrounded by a high wall, and no one dared to enter it, for it belonged to a witch of great power, who was feared by the whole world. One day the woman stood at the window overlooking the garden, and saw there a bed full of the finest rampion: the leaves looked so fresh and green that she longed to eat them. The desire grew day by day, and just because she knew she couldn't possibly get any, she pined away and became quite pale and wretched. Then her husband grew alarmed and said:

"What ails you, dear wife?"

"Oh," she answered, "if I don't get some rampion to eat out of the garden behind the house, I know I shall die."

The man, who loved her dearly, thought to himself, "Come! rather than let your wife die you shall fetch her some rampion, no matter the cost." So at dusk he climbed over the wall into the witch's garden, and hastily gathering a handful of rampion leaves, he returned with them to his wife. She made them into a salad, which tasted so good that her longing for the forbidden food was greater than ever. If she were to know any peace of mind, there was nothing for it but that her husband should climb over the garden wall again, and fetch her some more. So at dusk over he went, but when he reached the other side he drew back in terror, for there, standing before him, was the old witch.

"How dare you," she said, with a wrathful glance, "climb into my garden and steal my rampion like a common thief? You shall suffer for your foolhardiness."

"Oh!" he implored, "pardon my presumption; necessity alone drove me to the deed. My wife saw your rampion from her window, and conceived such a desire for it that she would certainly have died if her wish had not been gratified." Then the Witch's anger was a little appeased, and she said:

"If it's as you say, you may take as much rampion away with you as you like, but on one condition only--that you give me the child your wife will shortly bring into the world. All shall go well with it, and I will look after it like a mother."

The man in his terror agreed to everything she asked, and as soon as the child was born the Witch appeared, and having given it the name of Rapunzel, which is the same as rampion, she carried it off with her.

Rapunzel was the most beautiful child under the sun. When she was twelve years old the Witch shut her up in a tower, in the middle of a great wood, and the tower

had neither stairs nor doors, only high up at the very top a small window. When the old Witch wanted to get in she stood underneath and called out:

"Rapunzel, Rapunzel, Let down your golden hair."

For Rapunzel had wonderful long hair, and it was as fine as spun gold. Whenever she heard the Witch's voice she unloosed her plaits, and let her hair fall down out of the window about twenty yards below, and the old Witch climbed up by it.

After they had lived like this for a few years, it happened one day that a Prince was riding through the wood and passed by the tower. As he drew near it he heard someone singing so sweetly that he stood still spell-bound, and listened. It was Rapunzel in her loneliness trying to while away the time by letting her sweet voice ring out into the wood. The Prince longed to see the owner of the voice, but he sought in vain for a door in the tower. He rode home, but he was so haunted by the song he had heard that he returned every day to the wood and listened. One day, when he was standing thus behind a tree, he saw the old Witch approach and heard her call out:

"Rapunzel, Rapunzel, Let down your golden hair."

Then Rapunzel let down her plaits, and the Witch climbed up by them.

"So that's the staircase, is it?" said the Prince. "Then I too will climb it and try my luck."

So on the following day, at dusk, he went to the foot of the tower and cried:

"Rapunzel, Rapunzel, Let down your golden hair."

and as soon as she had let it down the Prince climbed up.

At first Rapunzel was terribly frightened when a man came in, for she had never seen one before; but the Prince spoke to her so kindly, and told her at once that his heart had been so touched by her singing, that he felt he should know no peace

of mind till he had seen her. Very soon Rapunzel forgot her fear, and when he asked her to marry him she consented at once. "For," she thought, "he is young and handsome, and I'll certainly be happier with him than with the old Witch." So she put her hand in his and said:

"Yes, I will gladly go with you, only how am I to get down out of the tower? Every time you come to see me you must bring a skein of silk with you, and I will make a ladder of them, and when it is finished I will climb down by it, and you will take me away on your horse."

They arranged that till the ladder was ready, he was to come to her every evening, because the old woman was with her during the day. The old Witch, of course, knew nothing of what was going on, till one day Rapunzel, not thinking of what she was about, turned to the Witch and said:

"How is it, good mother, that you are so much harder to pull up than the young Prince? He is always with me in a moment."

"Oh! You wicked child," cried the Witch. "What is this I hear? I thought I had hidden you safely from the whole world, and in spite of it you have managed to deceive me."

In her wrath she seized Rapunzel's beautiful hair, wound it round and round her left hand, and then grasping a pair of scissors in her right, snip snap, off it came, and the beautiful plaits lay on the ground. And, worse than this, she was so hard-hearted that she took Rapunzel to a lonely desert place, and there left her to live in loneliness and misery.

But on the evening of the day in which she had driven poor Rapunzel away, the Witch fastened the plaits on to a hook in the window, and when the Prince came and called out:

"Rapunzel, Rapunzel, Let down your golden hair."

She let them down, and the Prince climbed up as usual, but instead of his beloved Rapunzel he found the old Witch, who fixed her evil, glittering eyes on him, and cried mockingly:

"Ah, ah! You thought to find your lady love, but the pretty bird has flown and its song is dumb; the cat caught it, and will scratch out your eyes too. Rapunzel is lost to you for ever you will never see her more."

The Prince was beside himself with grief, and in his despair he jumped right down from the tower, and, though he escaped with his life, the thorns among which he fell pierced his eyes out. Then he wandered, blind and miserable, through the wood, eating nothing but roots and berries, and weeping and lamenting the loss of his lovely bride. So he wandered about for some years, as wretched and unhappy as he could well be, and at last he came to the desert place where Rapunzel was living. All of a sudden he heard a voice which seemed strangely familiar to him. He walked eagerly in the direction of the sound, and when he was quite close, Rapunzel recognized him and fell on his neck and wept. But two of her tears touched his eyes, and in a moment they became quite clear again, and he saw as well as he had ever done. Then he led her to his kingdom, where they were received and welcomed with great joy, and they lived happily ever after.

The
End